The Judge Jones Trilogy

by

Meryl M Williams

THE AUTHOR – MERYL M WILLIAMS born 1966

The author was born in South Wales and has written a number
of poetry books as well as another short story compilation.
She initially qualified as a laboratory scientist working both at
home and in the United States of America.   Since returning to
the United Kingdom, she has enjoyed giving poetry readings to
friends and family and has contributed to a local church
newsletter.

BY THE SAME AUTHOR

Mementoes in Verse
Reflections of Time
Doodles, Dog Ears and Ditties
A Boy's Anthem

Andrew's Amazing Odyssey and Other Stories

"The Judge Jones Trilogy" is a work of fiction and no
resemblance to any person, living or dead, is indicated or
implied. The author.

THE JUDGE JONES TRILOGY

CONTENTS LIST

The Judge Jones Trilogy

I. The Other Chair

Episode 1 – Judge Jones is Arrested

Not a single parking space was available at the City Court House. All the world and his wife had come to see the infamous Harry Skinner put away for life. Inside, the rooms and corridors were filled with bustling court attendants mingling indiscriminately with witnesses and members of the general public. There was an air of excited expectancy and the sentencing of Slashing Harry as he was known, was timed for eleven o'clock.

Judge Jones arrived, a little flustered, at a nearby side street where he attempted to park his car. All was going well, but Miss Shortley was mincing down the street in her high heels and seamed stockings. The Judge's attention was distracted momentarily and there was a loud crunch.

"Ya flippin' loony, what d'ya think ya playin' at", cried a voice.

"Sugar", thought Jones, "I've been caught". The voice turned out to be that of a purple headed teenager behind the wheel of an estate car which was now quite badly dented at the front.

"I'm terribly sorry", uttered Judge Jones, but the youth was not to be pacified. He continued to utter a stream of choice expletives and began to get close to the Judge, pushing him around. The scene was beginning to look ugly with Judge Jones starting to swear himself. Before he knew it he had landed the youth a choice black eye and the local Community Support Police Officers had arrived.

Bill "Badger" Davies calmed the seething youth while taking a statement in his meticulously kept notebook. The Judge by this time was furious and purple with rage but tried hard to be polite.

"Officer", said Jones, "I need to get to court to sentence a most hardened criminal. I really must get to court."

"All in good time, your Honour", answered Badger. "I just need to take some witness statements from the onlookers and then I'll deal with you. You look like you need to simmer down; you're in no fit state to lead the court."

A woman who had been standing by gave Badger a fair account of the entire fracas.

"It was entirely the old man's fault", she cried at the top of her voice. "He was so busy ogling the young miss that he reversed into the young man's car. I don't blame the young man for getting angry; his car's a write off".

"Now then", said Badger to the young man, "you need to exchange addresses for the purposes of insurance and then your Honour I am arresting you in the name of the law for actual bodily harm. You do not have to say anything but anything you do say may be taken down and later used as evidence in Court."

"This is utterly preposterous" spluttered the Judge. "I was defending myself against an attack that was totally out of proportion. Officer Davies please check your footage".

"Your Honour" uttered a woman police officer just arriving on the scene, "I need you to blow into this little machine."

2

Judge Jones was at least lucky here that he hadn't had any alcohol for over a week but even though the test was negative he was ushered into a police car and driven to the custody suite for an interview. The officers explained that he would have a chance to defend himself and would see a lawyer.

"Can I phone my wife?" asked Jones wondering what was to become of him. It vaguely occurred to him that he'd had no word as to the fate of Slashing Harry Skinner but that was not important now. No doubt Judge Mildew had stepped in to fill the breach.

Jones was shown to a cell which was quite large with a marble raised area covered by a plastic mattress. There was a hard, plastic pillow so Judge Jones rested dismally on the bed trying to come to some sense of his thoughts. But after years of legal experience he realised that he needed to plan what to say. His first duty it seemed was to defend his actions in being distracted by Miss Shortley. Clearly he had been totally misconstrued and an explanation was in order. He felt slightly heartened by the arrival of his supper, a small lasagne and a cereal bar, then settled down to wait.

Episode 2 – Jones' Lucky Break

Fortunately for Judge Jones, he was well versed in this sort of case and started his interview by bringing in Miss Shortley.

"Miss Shortley" he began "is forty-five years old and has been a serial shop lifter since a child. Her thieving has been small scale but long term, principally baccy and booze. I was distracted because of my dismay at seeing her in Court again. We really thought she'd kick the habit. It's hardly worth putting her in jail but she's lost her flat, her children are grown up and have children of their own and jail has become her only home. I am distressed by this case as I don't want Miss Shortley to die of hypothermia; neither do I want her to die in jail. Recently she refused to take part in Rehab insisting she has no problem. She is costing us a fortune."

Jones stayed calm throughout the interview then was allowed to rest. At three o'clock in the morning he was woken up to be told that the purple headed youth was positive for drugs and would be charged with affray; Jones was free to go home.

"I'll go in a taxi", he said to himself, "then Marj doesn't have to pick me up".

When the Judge got home he found his wife awake and trying to reach him on his mobile.

"My silly love", she said, "you need to stay in the car and wait until he's calmed down. What possessed you to lose your temper like that?"

"Can I get some sleep?" grumbled Jones, then he told her about the charges being dropped.

"I'm lucky I guess, but I have to go to court in three days' time to sentence Slashing Harry. I have seen just a touch of life on the other side and it's horrible. I know a good woman who tells me that criminals forgo their rights to human rights, it seems some people really believe that's appropriate. I can't sustain being part of this system but the first thing I'd like to do in the morning is sack Bill "Badger" Davies."

The shrill, strident sound of the telephone pierced the night air as Judge Jones reluctantly left a beautiful dream. He had been walking hand in hand with his wife along a golden beach with the waves of the English Channel lapping at his bare feet. In the dark he fumbled for the light switch, grabbing the telephone receiver.

4

"Sir, it's Badger", cried a familiar voice, "I've just arrested Miss Shortley once again; she's breached her licence conditions." Jones cleared his throat as he sat bolt upright, cracking his bald head on the eaves of his garret bedroom.

"But that's not unusual", he finally croaked, trying to find his watch.

"But Sir", answered Badger, "it's getting worse. It's six in the morning and Miss Shortley has just emerged from the Hoo Hah night club on Primula Street. She'd been drinking and has helped herself to four bottles of vodka from the all night off license. She came out with a stream of expletives and now she is locked up in custody suite."

"Heaven help her", uttered Jones audibly. "Badger you're right, we need to re-think this whole case. She's never cheeked an officer before and I thought she always stole baccy. Are we talking about the same lady?"

"Yes Sir", replied Badger, calming a little, "she is the lady often in court with the seamed stockings. We gave her strong coffee but she is singing her favourite song about lilacs." Judge Jones groaned inwardly as he reached for a fresh shirt. Then he spoke to Bill again.

"We will have to speak to probation. Miss Shortley needs to de-tox or she won't overcome her problems before we let her loose again, I have to give her longer as His Honour Judge Mildew always was far too lenient."

Jones replaced the receiver and sank back against the pillows. He really didn't want to get up but had to be back at court for the delayed sentencing of Slashing Harry Skinner and he couldn't possibly be late.

Episode 3 – Skinner Goes Down

The press had been barred from court for the delayed sentencing of Slashing Harry Skinner giving Judge Jones the chance to park in his own parking space at the Court House. Fewer people were around making the experience much less frantic and busy. His Honour was assisted into his robes while he consulted his notes consisting of his sentencing remarks. This was Skinner's fourth conviction for grievous bodily harm so Judge Jones felt it was appropriate to give a longer sentence that might actively deter him. The difficulty lay in one problem Harry had with alcohol. He described himself as a party animal and carried his knife with him wherever he went. The knives were confiscated every time but Harry persisted in obtaining them from his associates and from the Internet.

Judge Jones had consulted probation but felt that there were many factors that frustrated his genuine desire to help Harry. The defendant's computer had been confiscated, he had been barred from using the Internet but still his friends, possibly even his family, helped him acquire weapons.

"What we really need to do" announced the probation officer, "is make a succession of arrests to clamp down on the people both supplying Mr Skinner and feeding his problem."

His Honour sentenced Harry to four years with two of that to be spent behind bars and the remaining two to be spent under supervision on a license. In his concluding remarks the Judge spoke of Harry being cold, manipulative and a ruthless menace. Mr Skinner was taken down but the Judge's wife accosted him over supper that evening in their conservatory.

"Does it help anyone Darling", she queried "to pass harsh language like that? He will just get more and more angry and rebellious, feeling he has no hope of clearing the system, determined to 'show them' and just keep on doing it. There is no hope of a brighter future for Harry and it just brings down everyone who hears you". Marj left the house, taking their neighbours dog out for a walk in the local park. It was hard she thought to herself because her husband was a much kinder man than people realised doing a tough job in a harsh, judgemental, almost cruel set up. As she threw a soft ball for Rex, she suddenly spotted Miss Shortley in the distance walking briskly along the footpath.

"These are people too" she said to herself, "Everybody is someone's daughter or someone's son."

"Darling that's why you're a social worker and I'm a silk" grumbled Jones when she finally returned home. "If I listened to you, crime would go unchecked".

THE JUDGE JONES TRILOGY

II.Jones Returns Replete

Episode 1 – Jones Seeks a Respite

Marj was concerned about her husband's ill health but getting him to a doctor was a well-nigh impossibility. The Judge would grumble, fret, and say he didn't feel right but in the end did agree to a holiday at a local seaside resort.

"No fish and chips mind", Marj adjured firmly, "just lots of fresh fruit and veg. I'm packing the smoothie blender with my book of healthy recipes. We'll go self-catering then there will be no temptation to have fry-ups for breakfast."

"This could make me feel a whole lot worse" argued the Judge, "it's the fry-ups in the court canteen that keep me alive."

"No driving either", continued Marj, "we'll go on the train and go for some healthy walks along the sea front. Think of all that fresh air, maybe we could take in a boat trip or visit the local aquarium."

"Or the local hostelry", suggested Jones, "Brandy being medicinal, of course."

But he gave in because he knew Marj was right. Being part of the Criminal Justice System was very stressful and he was at the top of his game. Also he was finding himself more drawn towards his wife's perspectives and it would be a chance for quality time with Marj, putting the world to rights and learning from each other. In fact once he'd thought this through the prospect became more and more attractive.

"There is one problem I hadn't thought of", admitted Marj as they took the train down to Shining Sands, "the seaside is just as popular with our clients".

"I've brought my dark glasses", quipped her husband, "but I doubt anyone would recognise me without a gown and wig getup."

The lush, self-catering apartment overlooking Shining Sands Bay had a good sized lounge, well equipped kitchen and roomy master bedroom. On arrival, there was time for a spot of salad lunch then Jones suggested a walk along the sea front.

"It's a lovely day; this really was a good idea of yours Marj. October is often a nice month, sometimes we have the best weather at this time of year. Can we head towards those woods, the colours are just perfect." As they set out hand in hand towards Beachwood Glade the Judge said "I recognise the young lady sitting quietly on a deck chair, texting on her phone and munching a sandwich. I don't recall her name as it's been a while but I'm sure she's one of ours". As they passed he raised his baseball cap to the young lady and smiling, kept on walking.

"Well", said Marj "you're quite right, it seems you weren't recognised". This it seems was over optimism because as they passed by, the young woman spoke saying "Your Honour".

The Judge turned, meeting the young woman's eye directly and she spoke again.

"Your Honour", she repeated, "they didn't give me jail this time. I agreed to come down here to a drying out clinic. I've a roof over my head and went cold turkey; I've been a non-smoker and dry for three months now".

"Well done, I'm really pleased", the Judge said raising his cap again then he smiled and moved away as she responded to her busy phone. "I don't remember her name at all" he said to Marj as they reached the lovely woods "but it's a result we really need to achieve for Miss Shortley".

"Does anyone know her first name?" asked Marj.

"She won't use it in Court", answered her husband, "she must have quite a story but isn't much into talking. Never mind, we're on holiday now and am I not mistaken? There are some hazelnuts growing on that bush".

Episode 2 – Business as Usual

Back at the busy City Court House a new suspect was awaiting trial. A young woman in her early twenties was charged with supplying weapons, knives and also fire-arms, to a number of known cases including Slashing Harry Skinner. Kylie Smythe had not been in prison before yet had been in this business of her own devising for a number of years.

"If we can only stop this kind of seditious offense maybe we can make some kind of headway in the case of Mr Skinner", the Judge was advised by Detective Chief Inspector Frankley whose team had got their leads by following suspects on camera and through social media.

Judge Jones spoke generally with his wife that evening.

"If they commit fire-arms offenses", he explained. "They can't have sparklers or Christmas crackers on release. It seems like a petty cruelty to them but there are reasons."

"This time I can really see your point", replied Marj "It seems particularly harsh for Harry that no sooner is he out of jail again than this siren catches up with him. So we wait to hear what excuses she has, perhaps Harry is vulnerable."

"Without a doubt", said the Judge "he needs new friends which is very difficult. DCI Frankley and his team have made a good result though; that was challenging. This young woman is dangerous and so young."

Kylie Smythe was interviewed by probation as the officer compiled a pre-sentencing report. The defendant laid the blame for her five years of criminal activity entirely at the door of Harry and her other clients. In a web of intrigue she insisted that as soon as she tried to stop supplying weapons, her customers as she called them would keep on pestering her for more.

"Why are you blaming me?" she demanded of the probation officer, "when the government itself sells arms".

"That is a legal trade deal", replied the probation officer, "but let's not get involved with politics. Can you name your other customers and tell us who supplies you? Where did the fire-arms come from and who sold you the knives?"

Miss Smythe became defensive as she spoke again.

"You can buy knives in a kitchen shop", she replied, "but how do you know Harry got them off me?" The probation officer felt that Kylie showed not a shred of remorse, with no real feeling for the gravity of her offenses or sense of the wrong she'd done. Judge Jones, after consulting the pre-sentencing report and hearing from the probation officer in court, sent Kylie down for a year's custodial. Then he disappeared into the staff canteen, ordered a full English breakfast and took a seat alongside Michael Charles, the fine barrister defending Harry Skinner.

Episode 3 – Light Bulb Moments

"Tell me", Jones began "what does Harry enjoy when he's sober and not fighting?"

"He's an intelligent young man", replied Michael "and has been known to stay sober for months at a time. He has good literacy and numeracy skills but has previously held convictions for drink driving. Mercifully no-one has died".

"He's lucky then", insisted Jones, "but tell me, what can he do in jail that's positive? He has a long time to kill now, what's available to someone like Harry at Shooter's Hill for instance? It's miles from his home town but wouldn't that be good for Harry?"

Michael thought for a while before replying then admitted that Harry might not be allowed to do any cooking for a while but if he cleared the risk assessment there was beekeeping available at Shooter's Hill.

"They have a thriving shop selling honey and souvenirs related to beekeeping", he went on, "the offenders learn all aspects of bee husbandry as well as wild flower management and grassland ecology. Harry was quite taken with the idea, as he loves nature and wild animals and has no fear of being stung."

Jones returned home that evening to be greeted by a delighted Marj.

"That's a result", she announced "but I'm not so sure the full English was a good idea, never mind we'll let it pass; any news on Miss Shortley?"

"We've discovered her name is Jade. A friend of hers wrote to me and tells me that Jade is de-toxing inside with a view to attending recovery meetings. When you saw her she'd been allowed out on Bail. Judge Mildew gave her six months this time, recommending a strict programme of therapy. Let's hope it works."

"Well the news on the Home Front is that Claire and Samuel are planning to come home to us for Christmas and New Year. They have something to announce but won't say what. Can you have the time off in between as well?" she looked at him hopefully and the Judge smiled.

"Yes no question", he answered "we have a new circuit Judge who is covering for those few days".

THE JUDGE JONES TRILOGY

III.Jones Gold Standard

Episode 1 – Setting the Bar High

The Christmas and New Year holiday season was a peaceful and prosperous time for His Honour as his daughter and her husband came home from the Peak District where Claire was a country solicitor and Samuel was a male psychiatric nurse. The young couple were full of the news of Claire's first pregnancy, making it a very joyful family occasion. Judge Jones was relaxed and happy as he looked forward to the birth of his first grand-child in early June.

When Jones returned to his duties he heard from the new Circuit Judge that things had gone badly for Kylie Smythe who had spent her first Christmas behind bars.

"She'd got into a fight, been given a number of warnings and an adjudication, so I went to visit her to increase her sentence. It's not a task I relish", explained His Honour Judge Pemberton.

"The prison feel they have done all they can, but it's come to this", he went on, "but Jones, aren't you eating?"

Jones took his healthy packed lunch out of his rucksack.

"Edamame beans with rocket on malted bread", he announced, "setting the standard for the new baby. But getting back to Kylie; how is her English and maths?"

"Poor", replied the new Judge, "they are doing their utmost but she has refused to take the assessment at first. They will try her again next week after she's had a meeting with probation. Itseems such a waste of her young life but what they'll do is try and persuade her to use her time inside wisely. Really it's a golden opportunity for her to get an education and get on in life. You and I both know it can be done. Probation has agreed that we make sure she is not allowed to contact Harry again on pain of recall to jail".

"That's better", agreed Jones, "as he is starting afresh and we don't want anything to go wrong."

Episode 2 – Jones' Nemesis

"Have you heard the latest from Michael though?" queried Pemberton, as he wiped the last traces of fried egg from his plate with a piece of toast.

"Skinner's lawyer?" asked Jones, still munching on peppery rocket.

"That's right", continued Pemberton, "he is defending a certain Tyler Woodcroft who claims you gave him a black eye; a purple headed youngster; not quite seventeen, driving without a license or insurance and intoxicated. He comes before Mildew after the week-end and is charged with affray as well as everything else."

Marj spoke to her husband that evening exclaiming with some vexation how unfortunate it was that they lived in a small city where everyone knew everyone else's business.

"Will you be re-arrested if it turns out he really is a minor?" she asked him.

"In fact", said Jones, "Tyler's mother has come forward with his authentic birth certificate and he had recently turned eighteen. I have been arrested once when the charge was dropped even though I acted in self-defence as he was pushing me around. I don't know what Mildew will say to this young man but he'll probably get community service at worst. The scheme down at Marmouth is very well thought of."

Episode 3 – Jones' Last Case

"I may have to resign", Jones announced to his loving wife Marj over coffee in their rather chilly conservatory.

"It seems young Tyler wants to press charges in a private prosecution."

"Who's paying for that?" demanded Marj, "and will we have to downsize just as our family is increasing? What will we live on? Will I have to get a second job? What are we going to do? What were you thinking of? You thumped a teenager."

"He's an adult", responded Jones firmly, and he paced up and down gazing out at the snowdrops covering their flower beds.

"But I have to take responsibility", he went on, "I lost my rag and maybe it is time to quit. I have a generous pension, Claire and Samuel are both working; we'll survive."

Back at the busy Court House Mr Woodcroft, as His Honour Judge Mildew insisted on calling him, presented in the dock charged with affray. The older woman who had been at the scene spoke first. She did admit that the youth had been very angry but insisted that Judge Jones should not have lost his temper. As predicted, Judge Mildew sentenced Tyler to a hundred hours of community service and bound him over to keep the peace. But His Honour did tell the court that Judge

Jones should stand down as his behaviour was "not in keeping with his calling and was unprofessional".

Judge Jones went home to consult his case notes and the legal literature.

"I am not giving up that easily", he told Marj, "after all Mildew hasn't sentenced Tyler for using Class A drugs yet. That has been postponed until May. In the meantime we'll go flat hunting, how d'you fancy a seaside home?"

The Judge Jones Trilogy

IV. In Defense of Judge Jones

Episode 1 – In Endless Cycling

"It seems", said Marj, over breakfast in May as Claire was embarking on maternity leave and Jones was comparing annuities with life assurance, "that there is little love lost between you and Judge Mildew".

"Well", said Jones, switching off the computer, "he has achieved a good result with Jade Shortley and others but I was always more severe with my sentencing and he has been my severest critic".

"So the sentencing of Tyler Woodcroft is today, is it?" Marj asked.

"Yes it is this morning, but the charge against him is in fact supplying. He has obtained Class A drugs through his contacts then sold them on at a vast profit to some very vulnerable people. Even since he's been arrested there is talk of him getting involved with what used to be called legal highs; which are of course all illegal now. It is worrying to hear that as fast as they deal with one haul the traffickers find something else for scare and dare."

"Will you be in court?" asked Marj.

"No I'm not required", he answered. Then, he heard the post at the door and went to investigate.

"This letter", he announced as he opened an expensive, cream envelope, "is inviting me to stand as judge in the case of a much older woman charged with supplying a range of drugs to a chain of victims one of whom has died of an overdose. The victim leaves a young female partner and two small children." Marj reached out and touched his hand.

"I really think you want to return", she said, "Judge Mildew is quite a bit older than you, maybe you should just agree to disagree. He has obviously decided that City Crown Court really needs you. But you need an identity. Does anyone know your first name is Cedric?"

"No Marj", he said smiling, folding his arms across his chest, "I think they find Jones easier as its only one syllable. I don't mind being called Cedric but I had a sweetheart once who used to call me Ceddie. That is ghastly to look back on".

Marj giggled and spoke again.

"I wonder why it didn't last, seems it was fated not to be. But well done Miss, I wouldn't dare."

"Returning to the case of Mrs. Blanche", said Jones, blushing and abruptly changing the subject, "with your permission I'll email in and take on this little job as the hairdresser calls it. I will be in court after the Bank Holiday and I'll catch up on the latest gossip."

"Brilliant", cried Marj, "and next month when the baby is due Miss Shortley will be released. I'm keeping everything crossed."

Episode 2 – A Lesson for Jones

Michael Charles was on annual leave when Jones donned his robes for the hearing of the Crown versus Mrs Blanche. Her defense barrister was new to Jones as she had come from another area. Her name was Holly Herbert and she was particularly skilled at enticing her clients to tell their whole story. She was quite young but had a few years experience of specializing in cases of substance misuse.

Holly met Mrs Blanche for the first time at the Court House and noticed her poor eye contact which was very disconcerting. Also Blanche, who couldn't remember her own surname, had a spasm or twitch in her neck which she seemed unable to control. Holly was a kind, empathic listener and allowed a little extra time before sending Blanche back to the cell. The defendant told long, pitiful stories out of which Holly did her best to establish some truth. There were medical accounts that backed up some of the tales but not all Blanche's stories had details that added up. Some accounts of her home area were inaccurate, changing each time she spoke.

Holly persuaded Blanche to stick to the plan by making an early, guilty plea meaning her sentence would be reduced by one third. Blanche seemed all too aware that this meant she would get no trial but the evidence was stacked against her. The relatives of her dead victim had handed in their phones with messages from her arranging the selling of hard drugs. They had agreed to co-operate after the shock of losing their loved one who was under thirty years old. Blanche had experienced a number of abusive relationships with men, there were grown up children and she had grand children she had never met.

Holly spent time talking the matter through with Judge Jones before he met Blanche in the Court room. Holly was convinced that Blanche needed medical treatment, recommending a stay at a psychiatric unit for assessment and tests. Jones heard her out saying he would listen as she had been very thorough.

"I feel", said Jones "that I have to be strict as a very young man has died. Drugs devastate lives, those that quickly become addicted only see the knock on effects when tragedy strikes. But Holly you're right, she needs help and you've given her the best advice in pushing for an early, guilty plea."

Episode 3 – Blood and Tears

The wettest June on record brought the arrival of Marj and Cedric's first grandchild, a healthy boy named Damian as his Dad enjoyed reading Chaucer.

"Let's hope his morals are more astute", mused Jones cradling tiny Damian in his arms and marveling at the minute hands and feet. Claire was taking six months off work while Samuel returned to work after their short holiday at Shining Sands where His Honour had bought a flat. Samuel's parents visited from Derbyshire making up a full house with all the family fussing proudly over the new arrival.

After Claire and Samuel returned to their home in Derbyshire, Cedric and Marj took their favourite walk to Beachwood Glade as a double rainbow lit up the Western sky. Just as they were retracing their steps back to their Seaside home, a voice once again cried out "Your Honour".

"Who is it?" asked the Judge, temporarily blinded by the rays of the setting sun. The only answer he received was a hard blow to his back as he sank silently in a pool of blood with Marj beside him desperately trying to fumble for her mobile phone in her handbag.

As Marj dialled the emergency services she tried to speak to her husband who was unresponsive. Holding on to the phone with her shoulder she removed her light, summer cardigan and scarf using them to staunch the blood flowing from the knife wound in Cedric's back. She asked for Police as well as the ambulance, giving their location and doing her best to describe an attacker whom she said she had just glimpsed in the gloaming. Paramedics arrived on the scene and lifted Cedric onto a stretcher to take him to the Queen Mary Hospital which was at neighbouring Marmouth.

"He is still breathing and it looks as though the knife did not pierce your husband's lungs. Yes, do come with him and the Police will search the area for the weapon and any traces of the assailant. Is there someone you can call and do you live locally?"

Marj explained that they had a flat in the area but lived mostly in the City where she had a neighbour who could look after the house. She spoke randomly as the shock hadn't finally hit her but had to swallow her tears.

Cedric lay on his hospital bed while the nurse phoned Claire. The Judge's daughter was determined to come back to the area the very next day and spoke to her mother to reassure her that she would come by train and the baby would be well cared for by Samuel. The nurse encouraged Marj to get something to eat.

"It is critical", she said "but he is out of immediate danger. Your prompt action was brave and saved the day".

The Judge Jones Trilogy

V. Nine Lives for Jones

Episode 1 – We Love You Jones

Sitting at Cedric's hospital bed side, Marj held his hand and gently talked keeping her eyes on his face.

"Darling", she said, "our Ruby Wedding is very soon and we always talked of renewing our vows. I don't think I can get anywhere near my wedding frock anymore but I could order a pastel coloured outfit from our catalogue. You always loved me in pretty, soft shades. Modern hats are quite big and floppy but I could wear some lillies in my hair". She shed tears but noticed a tiny flicker of interest on her husband's face and his breathing sounded a little deeper.

Claire arrived giving her Mum a hug, giving the latest news on Damian and feeling sure her Dad would pull through.

"I'll let you have some time with your Dad", replied Marj and she took a break in the hospital cafeteria. Claire sat quietly with her Dad and talked over happy, childhood memories of camping and fishing trips. When Marj returned, slowly Cedric's eyes opened and the nurse gave his family more reassurance.

As Cedric recovered Marj spent time with Occupational Therapy to help put together a care plan that would get him back on his feet.

"Cedric enjoys concert going, hiking, fishing and the Countryside but also likes the buzz of City life. He will want to return to work and many High Court judges are still working after retirement age and it's a risk we all face."

His Honour Judge Mildew called at the hospital once Jones was sitting up and keeping his food down.

"I brought you some fruit", said Mildew, "and I'm thinking this could have been any one of us. It's good to know you've pulled through". Jones ate some grapes and then spoke slowly.

"The police have made an arrest but they couldn't find any link with any of my known case load."

"Yes", replied Mildew, "but you'd seen a woman who called out to you last October when you were walking along the Sea front with Marj. She did so well to stop the blood with her scarf and cardigan; that was lateral thinking. Well Jones, I for one really hope we see you back in your robes at City Court House as soon as you're ready. Pemberton and Michael Charles are coming to see you but doctor's orders are – no talking shop!"

Episode 2 – The City Beckons

When the hospital team finally allowed Jones to be discharged, Cedric asked if he could return to their house in the City.

"I'll take it easy", he promised, "but we can enjoy the conservatory again and I can improve my fitness by climbing the stairs. The flat by the sea is in a beautiful spot but it's on the ground floor." Marj drove steadily into the City and when they arrived they discovered that their neighbour had put the heating on for half an hour to take the chill off the house.

24

Roses were blooming in the front garden and the neighbour's son had mown the lawn.

Jones sat gingerly down in his favourite armchair feeling still a bit stiff from his injury and wondering if it would ever fully heal. Once Marj and Cedric had settled in for a few days, Judge Pemberton came to visit with Michael Charles. They brought the latest court room gossip about Holly Herbert who was doing well but at the expense of decorum. Well-advised by Marj they kept off the subject of their clients, talking of their own family holidays and the latest what's on news.

After they'd gone Claire phoned to talk to her Dad, expressing the concern that Shining Sands wasn't safe for him.

"You don't know Dad", she explained, "the unknown assailant might have been the same person you saw last October as Mr Mildew suggested. Mum will be going to the identity parade to see if it jogs her memory but is there no way you could remember that person's name?"

"I'd need to see my case file", her Dad replied, "but I have to go for some exercise and recover more before they let me. I have been approved a planned return to work."

Episode 3 –Results Come Through

"The pen" quoted Jones, taking his old seat in the staff canteen at City Court House, "is mightier than the sword and we cannot keep our clients silent or attempt to stop their mouths to fulfill our own ends. Michael what's the latest about Jade Shortley? She's been released again but is she surviving?"Michael was just ordering a new item on the staff canteen menu. The catering manager had called it a "Jones Special" and they were selling very well. The meal was a salad of edamame beans, rocket, lettuce and beetroot with new potatoes on the side and optional ham or chick pea fritter.

"Miss Shortley has been re-housed", Michael replied. "It's going very well so far. She had completed a course of therapy inside and is so far staying dry and out of trouble. Without the demon drink we've been told she's a lot calmer in her mood and more stable. She had received some support to contact her grown up children and we understand that's going well. But Jones, how is Marj, Claire and the new grandson?"

"Well Damian has fine lungs although is now sleeping right through so Claire and Samuel are coming to see us again for a week end in October. Michael, where is Holly? I have Blanche appearing in court again this afternoon for sentencing and I've seen nothing of her defense lawyer." Michael told him that Holly had stood down as she was finding court life very stressful.

"It seems", Michael continued, "that her mother has been unwell which compounded the problem. It's a shame though as she was really quite talented. But Blanche has been discharged by the psychiatric unit after covering a lot of ground with her therapy and groups. Our most senior barrister has taken on her case and we've heard that another death has arisen out of her previous activities. It calls for a tough stance Jones, I'm with you on that."

At the end of Jones first day back at the busy City Court House, Marj picked him up from the staff entrance and drove himhome via the park. She drove carefully, slowing down for the sleeping policemen and braking with care.

"I've had a very easy day really", he told her after supper. "But it's harder tomorrow, Kylie Smythe is facing fresh charges but let's enjoy coffee in the conservatory and put all this out of our minds. What date did Claire give us for their next visit and as the pen really is mightier than the sword where is that letter from Cousin Caroline in Australia? We could answer it tonight."

The Judge Jones Trilogy

VI. The Scales are Balanced

Episode 1 – Marj Protects her Own

Kylie Smythe appeared before His Honour Judge Pemberton who noticed that her hair was plaited whereas previously it had been quite short. A keenly observant man he also noticed that the tattoo on her neck was quite new.

"Home made" he thought to himself beginning to itch under his wig. As he took his seat, advising the defendant to do the same, a disturbance at his right occurred caused by a young man bursting into the spectators' gallery in a bid to influence proceedings.

"Kylie is innocent", yelled the young man but a bustling court attendant quietly and thoroughly insisted he remain silent and seated.

"Sir, please remove your hood", demanded Pemberton while the court artist drew the man's likeness. The youth was about the same height as Kylie with a clean shaven face and the Judge thought he could detect a resemblance. The young man sat down abruptly, pulling off his sweater and sitting sullenly in T-shirt and jeans.

"Your Honour" called the youth.

"Silence in court" thundered Pemberton smartly rapping his gavel. "Sir you will be asked to leave if you do not respect proceedings. Let prosecution commence." Prosecution read

28

out the charges, the latest being that the knife used to attack Jones had been found and traced back to similar weapons Kylie regularly supplied to Skinner and others. Kylie had pleaded not guilty and wouldn't budge on who the knives had been supplied to.

"You must return to court to continue your trial two weeks today", announced Pemberton. "I am advising your legal team that it would be appropriate in your case to come clean as to who is keeping you silent. A man has had his life threatened and these menacing weapons could continue to be used against yet more innocent victims. I urge you to spend the next two weeks at Fallow Fields Jail thinking over your contact list and finally submitting these people to justice."

Marj watched the news that evening surprised to find that the case of Kylie Smythe was amongst the headlines on the local programme. The artist's impression of the court room showed a picture of Kylie in the dock although the young man had been shown out by this time. Amongst the faces in the public gallery Marj was convinced she recognised her husband's unknown assailant. The hairs on the back of her neck stood up as she reached out a hand for the landline. She thought for a moment, the television programme switched to other news and with due consideration she rang the non emergency number for City Police.

Episode 2 –I wasn't there Your Honour

An arrest had been made, Jones was immensely proud of his lovely wife, but Pemberton was not satisfied.

"The evidence is flimsy and the defendant has a cast iron alibi", argued Holly Herbert back from a spell at Oxbridge University and more effective than ever. "At least three reliable witnesses have all asserted that Caitlin Moore was at the Hoo Hah Night Club on Primula Street on the night of the attack." Pemberton adjusted his wig after hearing the testimony of those three friends of the accused then called for Caitlin's mother, a very slick talker.

"My daughter arrived home from work at five-thirty that evening," she reasoned. "She had a bite to eat with the family then headed out to meet the friends who were with her. My daughter is learning to drive but as yet has no transport of her own. The train to Shining Sands takes an hour and Caitlin would have had to walk to Beachwood Glade from the station. No your Honour you have no case against my daughter".

"Marj I'm sorry but your memory must be playing tricks with you. But casting your mind back to that first encounter on the promenade Jones did you find anything in your case load?" Pemberton asked them after.

"It's an old case", replied Jones consulting his lap top. "Caitlin Harris came before me five years ago and here's her photograph. She was charged with Grievous Bodily Harm but the charges were dropped as she had a cast iron alibi. Her mother said she had been with her all the time and also spoke fluently in the court room on that occasion".

"It's too easy for them and she has a lot of background knowledge as to how long it would take to reach Beachwood Glade from the City", suggested Jones, "what perhaps we need to do is ask DCI Frankley when or if Caitlin changed her second name, did she book herself a taxi from the station or did she in fact take her Dad's car and drive on a provisional license?"

Episode 3 – Facing the Facts

Marj and Cedric decided they would renew their marital vows on a Saturday near to their anniversary that October when the whole family could be gathered together. Marj enjoyed organising select parties, their neighbours would be there and Cousin Caroline would be over from Australia stopping at their City home for a long week end before touring Europe. The knife wound still plagued Cedric with stiffness and a ghastly scar which he quipped he couldn't see as it was behind him.

"I can see how much it has healed though", said Marj, "and the ointment seems to ease the stiffness and soothe some of the raw redness. You are almost up to speed with our walks in the park but it's probably best to only go in broad daylight. It will cheer you no end to see the family and Cousin Caroline has been a great comfort with her emails and that nice letter."

DCI Frankley sent a message of support to Jones, wishing him many more years of happy marriage and including a short ending to say that Caitlin had changed her name after leaving her life partner just a year before the attack. She had returned to her parental home and further enquiries with the staff at the Hoo Hah Night Club were showing that the three friends were mixing their dates. But Pemberton was uneasy and called Marj as a witness. He gazed for a while at his lap top, poured himself a glass of water, then spoke to Mrs Jones.

"Magna Carta states and I quote", he began, "no man shall be unlawfully imprisoned without fair trial. Caitlin has been forced to plead guilty and therefore gets locked up with her sentence reduced by a third but admittedly the evidence stacked against her is insubstantial and circumstantial. Mrs Jones; could you have been mistaken?"

31

Mrs Jones was handed a box of tissues by the court attendant and paused also before considering her answer.

"Your Honour", she replied, "did the defendant catch a taxi from the railway station at Shining Sands to Beachwood Glade? Or did she drive her father's car on a provisional licence? Did she put in an appearance at the Hoo Hah Night Club? Was she with her friends after dining at home?"

"The fact is", said Judge Pemberton "that Caitlin Harris nee Moore was in the night club as she signed the visitor's book on arrival and departure. Her father was using his car himself to drive Caitlin's friend home after the evening was over and no taxi was booked to the woods. I have to ask you Mrs Jones, were you your husband's unknown assailant?"

The Judge Jones Trilogy

VII. The Axe Falls

Episode 1 – Fallow Fields Jail

Marj was to discover much later that the girls called the special transport van a sweat box. Locked into a cubicle with sandwiches and a small bottle of water, she reviewed the day's events.

"I'm not yet sixty", she thought, "it won't last that long and then at last I will be truly free." The van arrived at Fallow Fields Jail and Marj was introduced at reception. She saw the nurse who measured her blood pressure and found it to be a little high.

"Have you children?" asked the nurse.

"I fell pregnant at eighteen", mused Marj, "my College career in shatters. My daughter is everything I'm not and now she has a husband and child of her own. I married an older man at the dictates of an autocratic father and stayed in a prison of my own devising. Now I'm free for the first time. I was beguiled by him, he had money, position, silk lined suits but I can't imagine what he saw in me. He sought the ultimate traditional help mate. I stayed at home then did my degree by distance learning qualifying as a social worker once Claire was in school. It was hard to get work but I have done some. I lied to my own daughter about my age to conceal the truth and as for Cedric, he really believed the Caitlin Moore story; poor, silly Cedric."

"It's very serious", said an officer later that evening, "the charge is attempted murder."

Marj met a few of her fellow inmates over breakfast and did her best to avoid saying what she was in for, also she genuinely didn't know how long she was going to get. She was impressed by some of the girls in polo shirts who came to meet her with packs of crossword puzzles, colouring sheets and items she could obtain such as stress balls and puzzle cubes. The time went quickly enough and she met another girl in a different coloured polo shirt who explained that she would get an English and Maths assessment, after which she could do courses in art, cookery and horticulture from a whole list. Everything was a piece of paper it seemed but a few days later when Marj received her first reply she felt that she had never known prison was like this and wondered what her husband would say if he knew of her first impressions.

"He would just send people down and does he really know himself?" she wondered showing that their lives really had been very different with all Jones best points completely forgotten by everybody and Marj hoping to defend her actions that were really hard to understand. She fell into an attack of self loathing and self pity which she soon realised would have to be shaken off or she would go under.

"To be fair, he never laid a finger on me and was quite caring, even indulgent but he thought he could own me and I reached the tipping point", Marj spoke to probation who were stern yet fair.

"It's very serious", Marj was told, "and you could get a long time. You seem to show no remorse and we have no evidence of ill treatment. Your early pregnancy was fourty years ago and you were an adult".

Episode 2 – A Knock at the Door

Later that evening Jones made himself a hot chocolate, picked up the crossword puzzle and settled down before a warming radiator that was just coming to life.

"Is that you, darling?" he called as the doorbell rang, but unusually Marj did not let herself in. Jones put down his paper and cup then went to the front door, using his viewer. It was Bill "Badger" Davies with a woman police constable and they had removed their hats.

"We're sorry to disturb you, your Honour", said the young woman "but I'm afraid we have some bad news. It seems that Mrs Marjory Jones your wife has been arrested for the attack on your person that took place last June when you were out walking at Beachwood Glade, Shining Sands."

Jones was too calm at first but he took from them the proffered leaflet about victim support available in his part of City and then they quietly left him. Jones sat down suddenly feeling very, very cold and leaned against the radiator, now very hot.

"I'll email Caroline", he thought and he went to his computer in the lounge and did so straight away. He knew that Australia was at that time of the year around nine hours ahead so he thought to himself that he would check them again the following morning.

"I can't really work with this hanging over me", he thought. "I'll email Mildew to get him to take over", he decided "as he and Pemberton had done when I was recovering anyway. They haven't told me where they've put Marj. Will she be out on bail? Will they transfer her to another part of the country? I need a divorce lawyer and I can't ask anyone I know. I'll Google Spratt and Felixstowe to arrange an appointment;yesI'll do that tonight. I doubt they'll let me visit her and I think I'll finish the hot chocolate and get on the computer again".

Episode 3 – Cousin Caroline 'Phones

Jones awoke early once again to the strident sounds of his landline 'phone. This time he ignored the call and buried his shoulders deeper under the duck down duvet. The answer phone cut in and he recognised the mixed accent of Cousin Caroline.

"Ceddie darling", she cried in a loud voice, "I received your email just this morning. Its evening here and I was wondering if you'd like to visit once all this mess is cleared up. When do you give your evidence? Hope you're ok. Cheerio." She hung up as Jones leapt out of bed, sobbing bitterly over his first coffee of the day.

The storm of weeping subsided then Jones dialled Caroline's number.

"It's good of you to call Caroline", he said, his voice full of pent up emotion. "It's lovely that I can come and see you. I've got a legal appointment coming up. I'm just waiting to hear back from them. I'll just check my emails and once I've been to court I'll book the flight. Caroline that was really kind of you. What happened to Thomas? Wasn't he a landowner?"

"Thomas sadly passed away", replied Caroline, "yes the land is well looked after but most of the money is in trust for my great nephew. He's my only heir but I'm young yet, under fourty, we could have a child and daughters can inherit too. Come over Ceddie, put it all behind you."

The following few months proved long and wearisome for Jones as he waited for his divorce case to come up with his lawyers who seemed to move very, very slowly. Jones appeared at City Crown Court, giving evidence against his wife although he honestly stated that in the gloaming there may have been someone else there. He seemed to find some comfort from clinging to the belief that Marj was innocent of the attack and yet he was all too fully aware that he would carry through the divorce proceedings and move on with Caroline. Caroline had been his friend for many years and had settled in Australia when she felt that her beloved Ceddie just couldn't be prevailed upon to leave his wife. Now all that had changed and Marj was awaiting conviction as rumour suggested she would get around ten years, half of that a custodial sentence.

Jones put the doomed flat in Shining Sands up for sale and consulted his lawyers about the house in the heart of the City. Half of it belonged to Marj and its value had risen in the time they had lived there. But then Jones discovered his wife had had debts, the whole case was becoming messy and by the time the house had gone at much less its actual value there was enough to supplement his income, pay for the flight to Australia and give Marj an allowance for the time she spent inside. Jones sent an email to Caroline to tell her when he would arrive and realised that at last he was free.

The Judge Jones Trilogy

VIII. The Boomerang Effect

Episode 1 – A Ship Out for Marj

Claire drove out from her home in Derbyshire as the sun was
starting to light the Eastern sky. She was heading out to visit
her mum in Fallow Fields Jail after receiving a letter full of
news and events that Marj had been involved in. Claire had
not seen her mum in almost a year, she excused herself on
being unable to make the long journey with baby Damian
having a childhood complaint and what with starting back to
work and so on. It was a cold, clear morning and before setting
off Claire had checked her emails but there was nothing from
her dad who was enjoying a barbecue summer in the Southern
Hemisphere and had little time to contact his family. Samuel
had sent off photographs of the baby with his parents and a
short note of thanks had come through but little after that.

Marj was looking well, her daughter thought and after the
first awkwardness chatted freely about courses and crochet,
knitting and chapel. Then Marj asked the question that Claire
had been dreading.

"How is your dad getting on?" asked Marj and Claire
suddenly realised that her mum did not know where he had
gone to.

"Dad is visiting Cousin Caroline Down Under", said Claire,
"he'd gone for a few months as it's such a long journey. But

Mum I have discovered that there is a women's prison in my area, it's called Tawny Down and I wondered if you'd like to transfer there. Then I can visit you with Damian and Samuel as it's only a short drive."

Marj looked distantly at the bars on the window then turned to gaze at her daughter.

"They have asked me to stay here", she eventually replied, "as I am known here and I've settled in. But I'll mention it. It's a very long journey in the special van, I'd have to decide very carefully." As she paused an officer called five minutes and Claire realised that she had unwittingly upset her mother.

"It's alright", she said as she gave her mother a hug before going home, "I understand, your letter was glowing and you look very well." Then the officer called time and Claire had to go.

Marj thought long and hard when she was alone locked in her cell that evening.

"No", she thought, "she feels like a stranger now. As for Damian, he will probably never know, which is for the best." The next morning Marj was surprised that her probation officer was full of enthusiasm for the transfer. The young woman talked of family ties and said that it would be good for Marj to see her grandson grow up.

"It's a drive of just two and a half hours", she persuaded, "and you'll get a comfort stop. Just fill in an application form and ask the girls about Tawny Down. The food might be better."

Episode 2 – First Time, Last Time

City Court House was busy once again but Michael took a break from his case load, filed away his notes, and sat down upstairs in the roof garden with a ginger spiced latte. Holly found him gazing out over the city as the rain began to spatter on the perspex roof that covered the area where he was sitting.

"Michael", she said gently, "did the news reach you? I didn't want to let you know by email." Michael looked up from his reverie and spoke to her with a tone of quiet empathy.

"Yes Holly, I'd heard Blanche had sadly passed. It's awful to lose a client although she was older than some of our other service users. I'm sorry Holly, I'm glad you found me here. It's a dreary day and I was feeling a bit moribund."

"It's alright Michael, thank you for your kindness. On the other hand I have some really good news about Tyler Woodcroft. It seems he turned his life around and recovered from the drugs and alcohol. He is now living in his own place down at Marmouth and volunteers with the local task force collecting rubbish from the beaches."

"That's really good to know", replied Michael making a space for her on the bench beside him. "I am just thinking through the case of Kylie Smythe and strange to say I received a letter, beautifully written from Harry Skinner to say that he was enjoying the bee keeping down at Shooter's Hill and was eligible for parole. My colleagues at our City office have written back to offer representation and it really looks promising."

"You are feeling a little emotional at all this mix of news", said Holly smiling, "and the work goes on in force as Caitlin Moore has been re-arrested but for something else altogether. It seems that her father had been suspected of turning back the clock on motor vehicles for some time and she was complicit in selling them on. Also the young man who keeps causing a disturbance in court is related to Kylie Smythe and he comes before Mildew for a stream of charges that Kylie has always denied. But who was there on that fatal night Jones was stabbed and did Caitlin get there after driving on a provisional license?"

"Perhaps we will never be entirely sure", replied Michael draining his latte cup. "Pemberton has retired on the strength of it with a golden hand shake and Mildew is back trying to hold the reigns while Jones is replaced. I miss Jones, he had a wry sense of humour and will not see his child or grandchild now for a long time."

"Why Michael this is really moribund indeed", said Holly smiling again. "But Jones made his choice and is living the dream a long way from City Court House and its frantic case load. Let's head out to the canteen for a full English. Jones would be really proud of all you achieved and it's worthy of a celebration."

Episode 3 –Damian Walks and Talks

The special van weaved its way through traffic and started going more speedily when it finally reached the Motorway. Marj had a view of the surrounding countryside, seeing the distant hills of the Peak District with grey stone cottages and ancient churches off the beaten track. Then the van reached the portway of Tawny Down and paused before the huge gates were opened and they could drive through. Marj was in fact quite excited as Claire had promised a visit from the whole family as soon as her mother had unpacked and cleared the details her end.

"Damian is looking forward to meeting his Nana", said Claire once Marj could speak to her on the 'phone, "and Samuel is finding out what we're allowed to bring. Is there anything you'd like?"

"Just some more wool and another set of bamboo knitting needles", said Marj, "thank you that's lovely. Don't bring food or anything with glass but photos are very lovely. I can put them up on my notice board".

Claire, Samuel and Damian arrived for the Saturday afternoon double visit at Tawny Down and found Marj to be cheerful and happy.

"I've made a jumper for Damian which they should hand to you on your way out", she said, hugging her daughter. Damian was a little shy but began to play with a toy garage in a corner of the visiting area and was soon quickly absorbed.

"It's fresher here than near the City", Marj spoke to Samuel, "and I'm really glad I made the change. I've got a new job working in the prison gardens and I save half of what I earn. I have some money left for phone credit and some treats. Many girls spend like fun on canteen, buying chocolate and snacks but I am saving up in case I need money on the out. Do you know what became of the furniture from our city home?"

Claire and Samuel started speaking at once then Claire explained that some things had been sold but smaller items such as pictures and books were in storage in their loft ready for Mum's release.

"We are keeping them for you", interspersed Samuel, "and there is some money left over".

"It's my first and last time in jail", affirmed Marj "and I think financial hardship may partly contribute to the boomerang effect as girls struggle to live on their income, lose their homes and come straight back. It's not enough to say that people become institutionalised, it goes deeper than that. There are complex reasons for homelessness for instance and prison should not be seen as Society's answer. But that's the social worker in me and I can't tell you how lovely it is to see my grandson who is growing before my very eyes". Damian paused in his game with the toy garage and went to greet his grandmother addressing her as "Nana" for the first time.

The Judge Jones Trilogy

IX.   Bon Voyage Jones

Episode 1 – Modern Technology

The patio doors were open at Caroline's home in Australia as Jones relaxed with an ice cold beer, gazing out to sea where many wind surfers were trying their art.

"I've had an email from Michael Charles", he called out as Caroline busied herself preparing marinated chicken breasts. She washed her hands and stepped out to listen.

"He wants me to Skype him to see how we're getting on. He promises no case load of questions just a resume of how well some of them are doing. He also rather slyly indicates he's finally courting. The old dog has been on his own for years, I thought he was the ultimate committed bachelor."

"Wouldn't it be great", uttered the ever ebullient Caroline "to get an invite to the wedding."

"It's a twenty four hour flight", Jones reminded her.

"Well we could have a world-wide ticket and visit America", suggested Caroline, not to be outdone. "Or even go on a cruise." She returned to the kitchen while Jones agreeably pondered her suggestions.

"A cruise would be fabulous", he eventually responded. "I've got some savings and I received a bonus. But who in the world is Michael paying court to?"

"Some lovely lady lawyer, no doubt", giggled Caroline, "but will he make an honest woman of her?"

"That's a strong hint", cried Jones with a laugh, "tell you what Caroline, you can get married on board ship". Caroline snorted in disbelief and asked to see his decree absolute.

"It arrived only this afternoon", laughed Jones waving the paperwork just out of her reach, "but if we go on a world cruise you'll have to pay for your own ring. Why, is there no end to your demands?"

Episode 2 – Michael's Marriage

The computer screen flickered into life as Jones sat in Caroline's lounge, still sipping a beer. Michael's kind face appeared and he was alone in a small room at City Court House, dressed in his black robe with his wig beside him.

"Congratulations Michael", said Jones affably, "where is the wedding taking place?"

"Holly and I will marry at the beautiful chapel of St Hubert and St Joan at Largesse Cathedral; it's the church Holly grew up in. We thought we'd spend our honeymoon in China as we've always wanted to walk part of the Great Wall".

"Wow!" exclaimed Jones, sobering up for a moment, "that's fantastic Michael, you must be really fit. Are you planning a family?"

"Yes although it's early days yet. But how about you Jones? You look bronzed, healthy and happy. I can see the ocean behind you, it all seems very luxurious."

"It's glorious here", replied Jones, "and we too will be getting married but aboard anocean going cruise liner. We want to sail into Marmouth Docks in time to wish you joy. I'm

45

glad you got in touch Michael, how is Mildew coping without me?"

"We've a replacement coming soon", explained Michael "but Mildew is very experienced. He's an old hand who takes no stick although there certainly have been changes. Well Jones I'll say Bon Voyage as its morning here and I have to be in court. There's a new wave coming and we're glad to see you're doing so well."

Episode 3 – A Fresh Start

The fog had descended one chilly, autumn day as Marj stood outside the gate of Tawny Down Prison waiting for her daughter to pick her up. She had received an email from her ex-husband notifying her of his second marriage and wishing her well for the future. Marj had kept the letter one night then ripped it into pieces.

"It's done" she said to herself, "and I'm finally getting parole". As she waited for Claire to come, prison staff came into the jail exchanging greetings and wishing her all the best. Marj was to spend her first few days of freedom at her daughter and son-in-law's home then she was moving into a new flat at a nearby Spa town in the Peaks.

Jones was with Caroline his new wife back in Australia after their World wide cruise. They had docked at Marmouth in time to throw confetti over Holly, now Mrs Charles, and she was genuinely thrilled to see them.

"Are you coming back Your Honour?" Holly asked smiling.

"Not likely" laughed Jones, "far too stressful, but you look blooming. I'm glad Michael finally succumbed". Back Down Under, Jones was firing up the barbecue while Caroline prepared her speciality marinated chicken breasts.

"Did you see the English news on the Internet Ceddie?" she called through the patio doors. "It seems that a new lawyer at City Court House was stabbed in the back while out walking his dog in Beachwood Glade, Shining Sands. The attack took place in broad daylight but so far no arrests have been made". Jones paused, holding the tongs for what seemed like a long time and held his breath for a moment before responding.

"Marj is in Derbyshire" he said quietly, "we know that she's with Claire, Samuel and my grandson." He sat down by the computer and prepared to read the International news.